PAWSITIVE BEGINNINGS

LEIGHANN DOBBS

INTRODUCTION

Pawsitive Beginnings is a prequel novella for the Mystic Notch Paranormal Cozy Mystery Series. This is one of Willa and Pandora's first adventures. Before Willa knew the truth behind her eerily intelligent cat!

"If only Willa knew how to communicate with her feline companion, who happens to be privy to certain evidence that her human is not, Willa might find the suspicious happenings in Mystic Notch easier to understand. Mystic Beginnings brings supernatural together with classic cozy mystery, creating a plot that is just the right amount of creative and believable." Libybet R. G., Copy Editor, Red Adept Editing

CHAPTER 1

*L*ast Chance Books felt hollow and empty without my grandmother's presence. Sure, the store was much the same as it had always been. The same leathery-vanilla scent of old books. The same creaky pine floors, antique oak counter, and purple microsuede sofa. The same rows of bookshelves.

But without Gram, everything seemed a little less bright, and even though I was grateful to have inherited the bookshop, I was devastated that it was because of her death.

I might have felt a little guilty because I hadn't spent as much time with Gram over the last twenty years as I would have liked. After college, I'd gotten a job as a crime journalist in Boston, and as the years went on, I'd come back to my hometown of Mystic Notch, nestled in the scenic White Mountains of New Hampshire, less and less.

At least inheriting the bookstore had come at precisely the perfect time in my life. I'd just gone through a nasty divorce and was recovering from a car accident that nearly took my life. In my late forties, I wasn't getting any younger and was in need of a change and a slower pace of life.

I slowly made my way down the aisles of books, carefully running my fingers across their spines as I went. There were leather bounds, worn paperbacks, and jacketed hardcovers. Happy memories bubbled up of idyllic childhood summers spent curled up on one of the chairs, reading while Gram ran the bookshop, and I found myself relaxing.

As I turned a corner, I sensed someone watching me. I spun around to see a pair of unblinking, luminescent golden-green eyes brimming with curiosity and maybe a slight bit of uncertainty. It was Pandora, the cat I'd inherited along with the bookstore.

"Hey, Pandora." I squatted down and put my hand out toward her. She regarded it suspiciously then slowly walked over, allowing me to pet her. For as long as I could remember, Gram had had a sleek gray cat just like Pandora. In fact, they'd all been named Pandora too. I guess it was one of her quirks.

It surely couldn't be the same cat, because she'd be almost fifty years old now. Though I don't ever remember Gram without one. She must have gotten similar-looking cats as each one passed on.

"I think you should look out back, Willa."

The voice startled me, and I almost knocked over the bookcase I was squatting next to as I whirled around to see a wispy form appear.

Did I forget to mention that I also inherited two ghosts with the bookstore? Yep, Robert Frost and Franklin Pierce—that's right, *the* Robert Frost and Franklin Pierce—haunted the shop, and they were both hovering behind me with concerned looks on their faces.

"Out back?" I asked. You'd think I would be terrified to see ghosts, but these two were actually quite friendly, and this wasn't my first sighting. I'd been seeing ghosts since shortly after my car accident. Prior to that, I would have thought you were crazy to even suggest such a thing, but now... well... I guess I'd accepted that ghosts were real.

"Yes, there is something amiss," Robert said. "But please, don't take the path less traveled. I think you should go out there right away."

"You always have to work in one of your poems, don't you?" Franklin's ghost scowled at Robert.

"If the shoe fits," Robert said.

"Well, it doesn't fit, and besides, I think Willa prefers my books. They are in the front row."

The two continued to argue while floating behind me as I made my way to the back door. After owning the bookshop for almost a month, I was getting used to their rivalry about whose books were more interesting and more important, so now I tended to tune them out when they bickered about it.

The back door opened to an alleylike area behind the row of shops that Last Chance books was in. I opened the door, curious about what Robert and Franklin knew to be out here. Pandora must have been curious, too, because she came along right beside me.

I gasped when I opened the door. Someone was lying on the ground next to the dumpster!

I rushed over to the body, my heart racing. Who was it? Had they been injured somehow? Were they still alive?

I felt for a pulse, but there was nothing. The man was dead. A breeze ruffled his hair, and I recognized him. It was Bradley Eberts, the town's building inspector. I might not have known that had he not given me a big fat violation just the other day.

I frowned, puzzled by his presence. It wasn't even eight a.m. What was he doing back here so early? I was pretty sure the town offices didn't open until nine, and hardly any shops were open.

A door three stores down opened, and a woman with coppery-red hair stepped out. Marina Bettencourt, the owner of Mystic Spa, was holding a trash bag—like, on her way to the dumpster that now had a body in front of it. A crow which had been perched on the dumpster flew off, startled by her sudden appearance.

She looked at me kneeling on the ground, and a crease formed between her brows, then her gaze drifted to the body. Her green eyes widened, and she screamed then fainted dead away.

CHAPTER 2

$\mathcal{P}$andora had known long before Willa that Bradley Eberts was dead. She also knew something else that Willa didn't know. The little sliver of iridescent glass next to the body wasn't just trash from the alleyway. It was a piece of glass from an amulet. A magical amulet.

Bradley must have been wearing it, which meant that Bradley was probably one of the magical beings that inhabited the Notch. Pandora could see that Bradley was no longer wearing an amulet. Someone must have taken it. Was that why he was killed?

Pandora's previous human, Willa's grandmother, Anna, would have been on the glass like mustard on a hot dog. She would have known the small piece of glass that shimmered like moonlight on a lake wasn't like the ordinary bits of glass that littered the alley. Anna would have pocketed it and brought it to her friend Elspeth for safekeeping. Anna would have known that this death was no ordinary death.

But Willa seemed oblivious to the importance of the glass no matter how many times Pandora tried to shove it under her nose. So now it was up to Pandora. Because someone had to figure out what happened to the amulet. If it fell into the wrong hands, the results for the town of Mystic Notch could be quite disastrous.

Pandora reminded herself that she needed to have patience with Willa. The woman wasn't privy to the secrets of the Notch. She had no idea that some of the people who seemed to be mere humans were in fact magical. She had no idea that some of those magical beings meant to harm the Notch. And she certainly had no idea that Pandora was one of a group of ancient magical cats that had been tasked with protecting Mystic Notch.

It only made sense that Willa was more concerned with the dead body and the fact that the lady from the spa had fainted. Pandora was a little suspicious about that. She'd heard rumors about Marina Bettencourt and her facials that "worked like magic" to restore youth and beauty.

Was Marina using magic to produce those results? Most of the magical beings in the Notch hid their true powers, so it was difficult to know who was magical and who wasn't unless you caught them, and as far as Pandora knew, no one had caught Marina.

But still, was it odd she was here so early in the morning? The spa didn't open for hours yet. What if she killed Bradley and then slipped back into her shop so that she could come back out later and pretend she had discovered him while taking her trash to the dumpster? It certainly would be a shock to see that Willa had already found him.

While Pandora was musing about all of this, Willa had grabbed her phone and was calling the police. The police would come and scrutinize every piece of trash in the alley, including the magical glass piece. They might even take it and lock it away in one of their evidence bags. Pandora couldn't let that happen. She batted at the piece of glass, moving it as far away from the body as she could. Just to be safe, she shoved it into a crack in between the pavement and the building. She'd have to come back and get it later and then bring it to the rest of the cats so that they could analyze the magic.

Pandora and the cats of Mystic Notch could not depend on the police to help them. The police might be able to discern the human motive of the crime, but they were not aware of any magical undercurrents in the town. Making sure that magic remained on the side of good was up to the cats of Mystic Notch.

CHAPTER 3

$\mathcal{C}$alling the police was a little different for me than it was for other people because the sheriff was my sister, Augusta.

Gus, as everyone called her, showed up in record time, and I was surprised to see a flicker of concern in her amber eyes before she adopted her usual all-business demeanor.

Gus and I were total opposites. She was petite, with long blond hair and an hourglass figure. I was taller, with wild copper curls and a bit more padding. The only things we had in common were our amber eyes. We'd inherited those from our mother.

It wasn't that Gus and I were estranged. It

was just that we weren't too close, since I'd lived hours away in Boston most of our adult lives. I should have been better at keeping in touch with her, but I was trying to rectify that.

"What happened?" Gus asked as she looked over the crime scene.

"I came in early and found him there like that," I said, omitting the part about how the ghosts had alerted me to look in the back. Gus didn't believe in ghosts.

Gus immediately got to work, snapping photos and taking note of any evidence she could find. The EMTs had come and were tending to Marina while the coroner examined Bradley's body.

"Looks like a fatal blow to the head," the coroner said to Gus, who nodded. She'd already done a preliminary examination.

She turned back to me. "Did you see or hear anything unusual?"

"No." I wondered if Robert or Franklin had. If they had, could I relay that to Gus somehow?

"What time did you get in?" she asked.

"About seven."

She glanced back at the body. "Happened before then."

That made me feel a little better. I hated the idea of a murder happening right under my nose.

"I came out and saw her bending over the body!" Marina yelled. Apparently, the EMTs had woken her up. "Is she the killer?"

I glanced at Gus, who shook her head. "No, Marina, it's my sister, Willa. She owns the bookstore now."

Marina squinted at me. "Oh, right. Sorry, Willa. I'm just so shaken up about this."

"Don't worry," Gus soothed. "You're not in danger."

Marina didn't look convinced as she watched the medical examiner zip the body into a bag. "Wait. Is that Bradley Eberts?"

"I'm afraid so," Gus said.

"The building inspector?" One of the uniformed officers who was helping Gus raised his brows. "I bet he has plenty of enemies."

Gus nodded. "We'll need to start talking to those enemies and gathering evidence." She opened her notebook and jotted down a few notes.

My stomach dropped as I remembered the code violation he'd given me yesterday. Hopefully, that wouldn't lead Gus to consider me one of those enemies.

CHAPTER 4

When Gus was finished with me, I returned to the shop to find the bookstore regulars milling about the counter. The four senior citizens had enjoyed the tradition of having coffee with my grandmother every morning at the bookstore, and they'd decided to continue that with me. So in a way, I guess I'd inherited them too.

"Willa, we were wondering where you were." Bing Thorndike handed me a still-warm Styrofoam cup. Bing was about eighty years old but sharp as a tack, with bright-blue eyes and snowy-white hair. He was a retired magician and still had somewhat of a magical air about him.

Pandora trotted right to him, and Bing bent down to pet her. The cat purred and looked up at him adoringly as Bing talked to her like she could understand him. The two seemed to have a special bond.

"What are the police doing here?" Cordelia Deering asked as she took a seat next to her sister, Hattie, on the purple microsuede sofa. The octogenarian twin sisters were wearing almost-matching outfits. Hattie was in a pale-yellow pantsuit with a sky-blue blouse, and Cordelia sported a sky-blue pantsuit with a yellow blouse.

"There's been an incident," I said. I didn't want to shock them by telling them the incident was a murder.

"Incident?" Bing narrowed his gaze out the window. "That's the coroner's van. Would that incident involve a death?"

I should have known that I couldn't keep it from them. "Bradley Eberts."

Bing looked at me sharply. "Accident?"

"Not exactly."

"Someone killed him," Bing said it as if it wasn't anything too shocking.

Cordelia gasped. "Oh my!"

Hattie sipped her coffee. "It's not a huge surprise, what with all those building-code violations he was handing out to store owners."

Josiah shrugged. "He was always such a thorn in people's sides. I knew a lot of people disliked him, but I never thought anyone would kill him."

"Maybe not everyone will be upset that he's gone," Cordelia added.

"Do you think someone killed him because of the violations?" Josiah asked.

"It's certainly possible," Bing said.

"We heard down at the Cut and Curl that Bradley was supposed to condemn the building across the street." Hattie looked at her sister. "Didn't we?"

Cordelia nodded. "Yes, indeed."

We all glanced out the window.

The building was an old wooden structure that sat under a profusion of old oak trees. It had large windows and a front porch partially covered by overgrown bushes. Even though it could use a little sprucing up, it hardly looked like it should be condemned.

The building housed a plant store and florist named Petal Pushers. From what I could tell, the business was thriving. Despite the somewhat shabby appearance of the building, the display windows were always fixed up nicely with lush flowers and greenery and themed for every holiday.

"I bet Louise Franklin wouldn't be happy about that," Bing said. Louise was the owner of Petal Pushers.

Cordelia looked thoughtful for a moment before suggesting, "She could always look into renting another space in town. With her business skills and creativity, Louise could easily create something beautiful out of any old space."

"She doesn't own it?" I asked.

Josiah shook his head. "Nope. Dudley Chambers owns it."

I moved Louise to the bottom of the suspect list that was forming in my head and added Dudley Chambers. "So he'd stand to lose more than Louise if it was condemned."

Hattie nodded. "I don't know if there is insurance for that sort of thing."

I looked out the window at the worn wooden building and furrowed my brow. It was true that the structure looked run-down, but surely, it could be salvaged through some renovations. After all, Louise had put a lot of work into building a thriving business in that old space. "Is the building really bad enough to be condemned, though? I would think it would have to be inhabitable for that."

Bing followed my gaze. "Good point. Maybe that wasn't all on the up-and-up."

Josiah fiddled with the lid of his coffee. "You mean someone was paying Bradley off? I wouldn't be surprised—he's shadier than a hundred-year-old oak tree in the middle of summer."

Bing raised an eyebrow. "So, who would gain from having the building condemned?"

"Grady Dunn would." Cordelia reached down to pet Pandora, who had been sitting next to her as if listening to our conversation. "That's a prime corner lot here in town, and he really wants to put up a brand-new building for the real estate business."

We all turned in the other direction to look at Grady's office. It was a small space, sandwiched between the law office and the diner. It had been there for as long as anyone could remember, and it certainly looked like it was in need of an update.

"His mother is the one pushing him to do it," Hattie added. "Althea Dunn is always looking for ways to increase the family's wealth, and you know Grady. He doesn't want to disappoint Mommy."

That reminded me. Althea had asked me to order a book for her last week, and it had come in. I made a mental note to call her to come and collect it.

"Grady wouldn't have a reason to kill Bradley if he was paying him off," I said. "Unless Bradley refused to condemn the building and Grady thought he'd have better luck with the next person in line."

Everyone nodded and sipped their coffees thoughtfully.

"Well, looks like Gus has her work cut out for her." Bing stood and stretched. "I've gotta run. Hope this incident doesn't impact business for you, Willa."

The rest of the group said their goodbyes, leaving me and Pandora to reflect on the morning's events.

The whole incident must have tired the cat

out, because she wasted no time snuggling into the cat bed that I kept in the big store window.

I petted her for comfort. "Don't worry. I don't think we are in any danger."

Pandora slitted one green eye open then closed it again. She didn't look too worried.

As I got back to work overhauling the antiquated inventory system my grandmother had, my eyes fell on the violation ticket that Bradley had written up. It was a minor issue with the heating system. I made a note to get it fixed right away and pay the fine. I didn't need any reason for my sister to add me to her suspect list.

CHAPTER 5

$\mathcal{I}$ was exhausted by the time I got home that night. I was living in Gram's house, an old Victorian on the edge of town. I'd inherited that too. Gus already had her own house and job, so Gram had divided up her estate such that I got the business and the property and Gus got money. It worked out perfectly for both of us, and there were no hard feelings.

We were both happy to keep the house in the family, and I loved pulling into the driveway every night beside the big white house with its black shutters and farmer's porch on the side.

Pandora had slept in the passenger's seat

on the short ride home, and now she hopped out and followed me inside, glancing hopefully at the path in the woods.

"We're not going over tonight. Elspeth is on vacation," I said as I opened the screen door and let her into the old-fashioned kitchen.

Elspeth was as much a part of my childhood memories as my grandmother. The two had been inseparable. Elspeth lived in a gingerbread Victorian a few streets over, but there was a path in the woods that served as a shortcut between the two houses. I'd walked that path hundreds of times with Gram when I was little and recently with Pandora to check on Elspeth. Right now, she was visiting family in Massachusetts, and I had to admit that I missed her.

Pandora seemed to understand that we weren't going over there tonight and proceeded to trot over to her food bowl and meow.

I poured some kibble into her bowl. She immediately began to eat happily, ignoring me as she scarfed down her meal.

I wasn't much of a cook, so my fridge was pretty empty, but I managed to cobble together some cheese and crackers, which I took into the living room. My leg was hurting me—an injury I had acquired during the car accident—and I needed to put it up for a bit.

I settled onto the couch, resting my foot on a pillow on the coffee table, and turned on the TV. The quiet murmur of the TV in the background was comforting, and I began to nibble slowly at my snack as I mindlessly flipped through the channels.

Pandora trotted in and jumped on the couch beside me. It was comforting to have her warm body next to me, but she didn't stay for long.

She jumped onto the coffee table and batted at a paperweight that Elspeth had given me when I moved in. It was a beautiful piece—a clear-crystal orb that reflected all colors of light and reminded me of a crystal ball.

Pandora was fascinated with it. She batted at it gently with her paw, sliding it across the coffee table at me.

"Be careful, Pandora." I said, but I was amused by her interest in the paperweight.

She looked at me and then went back to batting it closer to me. She'd done this before, and the behavior was interesting. I picked the piece up and stared into its depths.

It was an intriguing piece of glass because it reflected things upside-down. Oftentimes, it actually seemed like it was showing me something that wasn't even in the room, but then I would realize it was because of the distortion from the round shape. As I looked in, I saw iridescent colors. That was unusual but must have been a prism effect from the lights in the room.

I put the paperweight down and yawned. "I'm beat. You ready for bed?"

Pandora trotted over to the stairs as if she'd understood. Truth be told, the cat seemed uncannily intelligent even if she was a bit stubborn.

I turned off the lights in the living room and followed her up the creaky stairs to my bedroom.

I brushed my teeth and changed into my pajamas then snuggled under the coverlet with Pandora sleeping at the foot of my bed. With the quiet of the country outside and the comfort of the cat purring softly, I soon fell into a deep sleep.

PANDORA WAITED PATIENTLY for Willa to be fast asleep, then she snuck out of the bedroom and down to the basement, where she had a secret escape route.

It was dark, and the moon shone bright through the trees. She followed the path she knew so well, past the old oak tree with the knothole she used to climb through when she was a kitten and over the stone wall. She hurried through the woods, listening the owls hooting and the leaves rustling as she took a shortcut to town.

She arrived at the spot where she'd hid the shard of glass and quickly retrieved it. Then she headed to Elspeth's barn, where the other cats of Mystic Notch hung out.

The big barn doors were open just a smidge, allowing a sliver of moonlight to illuminate the wide, worn wooden floors of the barn. Pandora slipped in and hesitated just inside the door, letting her eyes adjust to the darkness.

The barn was warm and comforting. The old boards were rough under her paws. The scent of hay and horses tickled her nose, though the horses that used to take up residence here were long gone. Now the barn was only home to the cats, and there were plenty of them.

"Pandora, what have you brought us?" Inkspot, the large black cat who was the leader of the group, hopped onto a bale of hay. His yellow eyes glowed in the moonlight.

Pandora dropped the glass, which she'd carried in her mouth all the way there. It glittered in the moonlight, casting a rainbow of colors around the group.

The cats all gathered around the shard of glass, fascinated by its ethereal glow.

"This is magical. I can feel it," Snowball meowed, her white fur standing on end. She stalked around the glass, looking at it from all angles.

"What does it do?" Tigger purred, reaching out to touch the glass gently with his paw.

"I'm not sure." Pandora hadn't quite figured out what it was for yet. "I found it near the body of Bradley Eberts."

Inkspot's paws thudded on the floor as he jumped down from the bale of hay. "It's a piece of an amulet. Eberts must have been wearing it." Inkspot circled the shard, sniffing and twitching his whiskers. "It's a magic amplifier."

"That's right. Whatever magic the wearer wants to create is amplified," Otis, the fat calico, said. Since only one out of every three thousand calico cats was male, Otis was quite rare. The problem was that he knew it and acted snooty about it. He had been a thorn in Pandora's side since the beginning. He was one of the old souls that had been around for centuries. Pandora was a newer soul with new ideas. For some reason, Otis felt threatened by these ideas.

"So it's a good assumption that whoever killed Eberts and took the amulet is magical," Pandora said.

"Indeed." Otis licked his paw. "Does your human have any ideas?"

Pandora held in a hiss. Otis had been teasing her about her inability to communicate with Willa. "She has some, but she is new to town so doesn't know all the players."

"I'm sure Pandora will manage to work with Willa. In the meantime, we need to figure out who would want the amulet." Inkspot's voice took on an ominous tone. "Because if the person who took it intends to amplify evil magic, that does not bode well for any of us."

"But where do we start?" Snowball asked.

"I say we start by looking for the people who have a grudge against Eberts," Tigger meowed.

"I overheard the humans talking about that." Pandora relayed the conversation that Willa had had with Bing and the others.

"That gives us plenty to check out." Inkspot turned to Pandora. "Did you notice who was around the area? Anyone or anything unusual?

"Marina Bettencourt fainted when she saw the body then asked if Willa had killed him!" Pandora said.

Inkspot's eyes narrowed. "That sounds a little over the top. Maybe she has something to hide."

"I've heard the female humans say her facials are magical." Snowball rubbed her paw along her whiskers. "Maybe she wants to make them even more magical."

"I agree. Sounds like we have a few suspects to check out. Let's meet back here tomorrow night and discuss our findings." Inkspot looked at each of the cats in turn.

The cats all nodded in agreement, their eyes glowing with determination. Together, they would find out who had killed Bradley Eberts and taken his powerful amulet. And they would stop them before it was too late.

CHAPTER 6

The next morning, I stopped at the town hall before I opened the bookstore. I wanted to pay the fine as soon as possible lest someone suspect me of having killed Bradley. It didn't escape me that he'd been right behind my store when he was killed.

Pandora seemed exhausted. She was curled up in the passenger seat and barely batted an eye at me as I parked in the town lot and told her to sit tight.

The town hall wasn't a grand building, just a simple brick structure that dated back several hundred years. It had large windows and a glass door whose copper doorknob was

smooth from generations of townsfolk opening it.

Inside, it smelled of wood polish and
paperwork. My footsteps sounded hollow on
the marble floor as I walked the hallway lined
with old maps and faded photographs of the
town's leaders.

Two women were behind the desk at the
town offices. I'd met them both before on my
various visits to become established with the
town.

Marjorie Evans was a sharp-featured
woman with dark hair pulled back in a tight
bun. She wore rimless glasses and had a no-
nonsense demeanor, her face etched with
wrinkles from years of squinting at paperwork.
Stephanie Miller was the opposite. A dainty,
young woman, she had light-brown hair that
she wore in a braid down her back, her face
was free of wrinkles, and her green eyes
sparkled with youth.

"Morning, Willa. Can I help you?" Marjorie
spoke with a clipped tone and exuded an air of
competence and authority.

I held up the violation paper. "I want to pay

this. I've hired someone to fix the problem, and they're coming on Thursday."

Marjorie took the paperwork and my check and squinted at it then handed it to Stephanie. The two women exchanged a glance.

"Gonna be a while before we can send someone out to reinspect, considering what happened," Marjorie said as Stephanie looked through a stack of papers.

"Yes, I'm so sorry about that. Must be hard on you guys, having worked with Bradley," I said.

Marjorie shrugged. "We weren't that close."

"Hmmm... this is number three-seven-four-five," Stephanie said. "But three-seven-four-four isn't in yet."

Marjorie looked something up. "That one was from Mystic Spa. It's overdue."

Marina had a violation too? That was interesting. I remembered how she'd been so shocked to see Bradley there that she'd fainted. I mean, I guess it was shocking to see a dead body—I suppose my career as a crime reporter had hardened me to that. My old instincts kicked in. She would certainly be a suspect.

What had she even been doing there that early? Surely, she didn't have a client before eight a.m.? A peek at her client register was in order.

"Oh, I wanted to double-check that there weren't two for Last Chance Books." Stephanie looked at me apologetically. "Sometimes, people get confused when they have more than one to pay."

"Thankfully, I only had one," I said.

Stephanie stamped a bunch of papers and handed them over the counter to me. "Okay, all set. We'll let you know when we can send someone out."

As I headed back down the hall, a commotion in one of the rooms caught my attention.

I peered into the room and could see rows of shelves lined with large blueprints and maps. There was a table in the center with a blueprint unrolled. A group of people was gathered in front of the table, pointing at various spots on the documents.

"That building is not bad enough to be condemned!" The shrill voice came from Louise Franklin. We hadn't met formally, but I recognized her from seeing her across the street.

"Calm down, Louise," a man said. I wasn't sure who he was—apparently, someone from the planning committee. "Bradley made a good case for it, but we can send someone out to reassess. He was the only one who looked at it."

"Well, you should." Louise huffed, crossing her arms over her chest. "Bradley didn't know what he was talking about. If you ask me, maybe he was being paid off to exaggerate the problems with the building. I should know. I've had my business there for years."

The man sighed. "That's a strong accusation, Louise."

"Right, well, I guess if you are willing to revisit it, I'll just have to wait and see what happens."

They both glanced at the door, and I waved and then hurriedly moved on. That was interesting—Louise certainly seemed upset about the prospect of having to move her business, and now with Bradley out of the way, she might not have to move at all.

CHAPTER 7

$\mathcal{I}$ got to the bookstore in time to catch the regulars. Even though I'd opened up a bit late, they'd waited for me and even brought me a coffee. It was heartwarming until they started to pepper me with questions and I realized they only wanted to know more about the murder.

"Does Gus have any suspects?" Hattie asked from her spot on the couch.

"Not that she's sharing with me," I replied. I got the distinct impression Gus wanted me to butt out. Not that I was trying to butt in. Okay, well, maybe I was, but I was trained to butt in, and the guy had died behind my store, and I'd discovered him. I felt a bit invested in the situation.

"What about you? Who do you think did it?" This from Cordelia, who was perched on the edge of her seat, eager for any gossip. Today, the twin sisters were wearing floral ensembles in matching peach and teal.

I shrugged. "I haven't really given it much thought."

"Meow!" Pandora piped up from where she'd been snoozing in her cat bed in the window as if she knew I was lying.

A car pulled up outside, and Bing's eyes widened. "Speak of the devil."

I looked outside to see the Mystic Notch Sheriff vehicle with its big brown star on the side.

"What's Gus doing here?" I asked.

"Maybe she's here to arrest you," Hattie said with a smirk.

I laughed. "I doubt that." Though I wasn't entirely sure.

We watched as Gus stormed toward the store, her long blond ponytail whipping around behind her. She pulled the door open and stomped inside. Her narrow-eyed gaze fell on Bing, Josiah, Hattie, and Cordelia.

"Don't you folks have something you should be doing?" She looked at her watch.

Bing stood. "Yep, I'm just heading out for a game of golf."

Josiah crumpled his Styrofoam coffee cup. "I'm heading over for chess at the post office."

"We're late for our appointments at the Cut and Curl." Hattie pulled Cordelia up from the couch, and they hurried out the door behind Bing and Josiah, casting me a sympathetic glance behind Gus's back.

"What's up?" I asked. Pandora must have been interested, too, because she'd hopped out of the cat bed and was sniffing at Gus's shoes.

Gus glanced down at Pandora, who purred and rubbed against her legs, leaving a trail of gray fur on Gus's perfectly pressed dark-brown pants.

"Why didn't you tell me that Bradley Ebert wrote you up for a code violation?" she said, her voice cold.

"Oh," I said, taken aback by the anger in her tone. "I didn't think it was that big of a deal."

But Gus's tight expression told me that I was wrong. Her eyes flashed as she fisted her hands on her hips. "You didn't? The man ended up dead outside your store!"

"Well, I didn't kill him. I think it's a little far-fetched that someone would kill the guy over a fifty-dollar violation, don't you?"

"Mew," Pandora piped in.

Gus glanced down at her and sighed. "I suppose. I was just surprised, when I looked through his work log, that you didn't mention it yesterday."

"Look, I'm sorry. It was a shock to find him, and then you were busy processing the scene."

Gus gnawed her bottom lip. "Right. Sorry. It's just that this case is important. We don't get a lot of murders here, and I'm not used to investigating. I don't want to have to call in help from the sheriff over in Dixville Notch."

I felt sympathy bloom in my chest. I could understand her frustration and her desire to solve the crime on her own. I'd been in the same position when I was working as a crime journalist. "Don't worry. We'll figure out who did it."

Her eyes narrowed. "We? I don't think this

is something you should be messing in. You're not a crime journalist anymore."

Was she saying that because she didn't want my help or because she didn't want me to endanger myself? It was hard to tell with Gus.

"I paid the fine, and the problem will be fixed soon. It was the heating-system controls. But when I was at the town hall, they said he had an outstanding one that hadn't been paid. That one was from Mystic Spa."

"I know that," Gus said.

"Well, don't you think Marina was acting kind of strange yesterday morning? She was pretty quick to blame me, and what was she doing here so early, anyway?"

Gus's lips tightened. "Whether or not I think she was acting strange is not really your concern. Your concern is staying out of police business and letting me find Bradley's killer. Got it?"

She took a step closer to me, and I nodded. Just like when we were kids and she'd try to boss me around. I guess it still worked.

A slight smile played on her lips. "Good." She whirled around and headed for the door. "Try to stay out of trouble today."

Pandora and I watched her drive away. Stay out of trouble? How could I when she made it sound like I was a suspect? Besides, it wouldn't hurt if I investigated just a teeny tiny bit. It sounded like she needed my help whether she wanted to admit it or not.

I looked down at Pandora. "I think I feel the need for a facial. What do you think?"

She turned her face up to mine, and I swear she nodded her head. "Mew!"

CHAPTER 8

The Mystic Spa was in an old building much like my bookstore. It was clean and bright, with antique oak wood adding a warm ambiance to the space. As soon as I opened the door, my nostrils were hit with an aromatic blend of fruits and flowers combined with a fresh hint of mint and lavender.

The check-in desk was gleaming white, and there were hanging baskets and potted plants everywhere, giving the place a fresh, vibrant ambiance.

"I'll be out in a sec!" Marina called from the back. The bell on the door had announced my arrival.

I looked around at the pamphlets on the desk while I waited and saw that they offered everything from facials and massages to waxing services. I perused the list of facials and saw that they highlighted several antiaging options.

Movement out the window caught my eye. Was that Pandora? But it couldn't be. She was locked in the bookstore and snuggled in her bed. I moved closer to the window but didn't see anything out there.

Marina appeared from the back room. "Welcome! What can I do for you today?" her smile dimmed when she recognized me.

"Hi. I just came over to see if you were okay, after..." I pointed to the back where Bradley had been found.

Marina flushed and averted her gaze. "I'm fine but rather embarrassed," she confessed.

"Don't be," I said. "It's very startling to see someone like that."

"It sure is."

"Did you know Bradley well?" I spied a sign-in book on the corner of the desk and inched toward it, hoping to at least see something from yesterday morning.

"No, I didn't." Marina flipped the book closed. Darn! Was she trying to hide something?

"But you must have known him from your inspection." I looked around as if making sure no one could overhear even though it was obvious no one else was there. "He slapped me with a violation the other day, and I heard he was in here, too. If you ask me, he was kind of hard on me."

Marina's face relaxed. "I know, right? I thought the one I got was unwarranted. I'm appealing it because it was stupid. Who cares if my wax was one degree hotter than it's supposed to be?"

"Mine was for my heating controls," I said. "Makes me wonder who else he wrote up with worse infractions."

Marina glanced out onto Main Street. Her store was across from the real estate office. "I heard him arguing with Grady Dunn across the street just last week."

"Oh? Does Grady own that building? I thought he wanted to tear down the place that the florist is in and build something new there?"

Marina wrinkled her nose. "And displace Louise? That would be terrible for her. I don't think Grady would do that. He's usually very nice. Was sweet as pie to me when I bought the old Donnelly place."

I cocked my head. "The old Donnelly place? That's your house?" The antique saltbox was on one of the main roads, and I'd always loved the giant old oak trees in the yard.

Marina nodded, a pleased smile on her face. "Yes, it is. It was built in the early 1700s, but it's in good condition with many original features."

"It looks well cared for."

"It's a great house. In fact, the previous owners even wanted to buy it back. They implied that they didn't mean to sell it and Grady had scammed them into it somehow." Marina shook her head. "Typical seller's remorse."

"How strange. So, what were Bradley and Grady fighting about?" I asked to steer the conversation back on track.

"I have no idea. I could hear loud voices but not what they were saying." Marina shrugged. "Anyway, what can I sign you up for? The pumpkin face mask is very soothing for dry skin. Or maybe you'd like a facial that is a bit more invigorating, like the mint puree?" She looked at me expectantly.

I glanced down at the pamphlet. "There are so many choices. I'll have to mull it over and get back to you."

"Okay, well, nice chatting, and again, I'm sorry about the other morning."

"No problem." I exited with my pamphlet and watched for Pandora as I walked back to the book store. Of course, she was sleeping in her cat bed in the window just where I'd left her. There was probably another gray cat in town that I'd seen outside.

PANDORA HAD JUST GOTTEN SETTLED in her bed in a fake sleep pose when Willa unlocked the door. Her heart was beating fast at what she'd seen when peering into the windows at the Mystic Spa.

"Did you have a nice sleep?" Willa petted the top of her head, and Pandora stretched lazily to feed into Willa's assumption that she'd been snoozing.

It was true that she had a secret escape spot at Last Chance Books just like she did at home. Both Anna and Willa were always trying to protect her, thinking it was dangerous for her to be out wandering by herself. They had no idea how capable she was of taking care of herself. It was the humans who were weak and needed protection.

Willa got busy stocking books, and Pandora's thoughts drifted to what she'd seen in the back room of the spa.

A woman had been lying in one of the comfortable chairs with a green goopy mask on her face. Why humans thought that was pleasurable, Pandora had no idea. She would hate to have that goop on her fur. Then again, since they were without fur, they seemed to put an inordinate amount of care into their bald faces. At least, some women did.

As Pandora watched this one, the mask started to glow, and swirls of magic drifted off it. The mask was enchanted, which meant Marina was definitely a witch. Pandora bet she would love to get that amulet and use it to amplify her magical face masks.

Hopefully, she was the killer and this was just about Marina wanting to deliver over-the-top service to her spa clients. Because if someone had a more nefarious purpose for the amulet, Pandora didn't want to imagine the consequences.

There was only one problem. When Pandora had looked into the back window, Marina had been bending over the woman, and she was certain there was no amulet dangling from her neck. But maybe she had it in her pocket. It probably wouldn't be a good idea to prance around town wearing an amulet you stole off of someone you murdered.

As Pandora pondered this, she stared over at Petal Pushers across the street. The porch was loaded with lush, healthy plants growing in window boxes and pots. Tangled vines crept up the walls and curled around the paint-chipped support posts. The plants grew so quickly that she could practically watch the tendrils of the plants getting longer and the leaves unfurling.

There were also several floral arrangements

brimming with vibrant flowers in every color imaginable. The sunlight cascaded down on them in soft rays, intensifying the colors even further, and she could practically smell their sweet perfume.

As she watched, a familiar cat appeared around the corner of the building. There was no mistaking the fluffy white Persian—Snowball. She looked over at Pandora, and Pandora nodded a greeting.

Snowball jerked her head toward the back in an indication for Pandora to join her. Then she nodded again and trotted off behind the building.

Pandora glanced around. Willa was busy with the books. Could she sneak out and get back before Willa got suspicious?

I had just gotten done leaving a message for Althea to tell her that her book had come in when Gus burst in through the front door. She always seemed to come in like a whirlwind.

"Don't you ever just walk in calmly?" I asked her.

She frowned. "What's wrong with the way I walk in?"

"You're always so forceful and abrupt," I told her.

She shrugged. "I'm trying to catch a killer. I don't have time to tippy-toe around."

"So, what are you doing here? Unless you think I'm the killer." She didn't, did she?

Gus gave me an exasperated look. "Of course not, Willa. I'm here looking for a necklace. Bradley Eberts's wife said he was wearing some funky necklace that he'd found in one of the old houses he inspected, but it wasn't with his effects."

I frowned. "Oh. I didn't see a necklace out back, but then, I was a bit distracted with the body and all. What's it look like?"

Gus screwed up her face. She wasn't one for jewelry. "She said the pendant was about an inch long and some kind of shimmery glass. Blue and green."

"I think I would have noticed, but do you want to take a look out back? Maybe it rolled under the dumpster or something." I started toward the back door. "I would think your guys would have found it, though."

"You'd think. If I find it back there, someone is going to be in trouble. As it is, the wife is making a big fuss, saying we stole it."

I winced. I could see why that would be a problem for Gus. As the sheriff, she took her job seriously, and I knew the accusation of someone in her department stealing things would cut deep.

The back alley was a bit dirty, the dumpster oily and smelly.

"Ew," Gus said, recoiling. "What is that smell?"

"Probably whatever is rotting in there." I gestured at the dumpster, trying not to breathe through my nose.

Gus got on the ground and shined her flashlight under it. "Nothing under there." She got up and brushed off her pants. "Let's check the corners and near the buildings."

We spent the next twenty minutes covering every inch of space but didn't find the necklace. I could see the frustration on Gus's face as we went back inside.

"Thanks for helping me look." She leaned against the counter and brushed more dirt from her uniform. Her eyes fell on the pamphlet from the spa that I'd left on the counter, and her expression immediately turned suspicious. "I didn't know you were into facials."

"There's always a first time." I pretended to stack some books so as to avoid eye contact.

"Really? Or were you over there snooping?"

Darn. I should have known better than to

leave that out in the open. "I was not snooping," I protested.

"Uh-huh." Gus didn't look convinced. "Need I remind you that you aren't a journalist anymore?"

No one needed to remind me of that, but it did make me mad that Gus thought my help wasn't worth much. I still had the skills even though I didn't have the job. "I did find out something that you might find interesting."

Her gaze narrowed. "What?"

"Marina said that Bradley and Grady Dunn had a big argument the other day."

"About what?"

"She couldn't tell, but she heard them from inside her spa. Said they sounded mad at each other."

Gus acted like that wasn't of interest, but I could tell that I'd told her something she didn't know.

"Well, you can stop snooping around at the spa." Gus tapped the pamphlet with her index finger. "She's not the killer. I hope you're not trying to get back at her for asking if you did it."

"Of course not. But how do you know she isn't the killer?"

"She had a client in her spa at the time of death. Has early appointments for a special client a few days a week."

"Oh." I didn't want to press my luck by asking if Gus had verified it with the client. She was pretty thorough, so I was sure she must have.

Gus pushed off the counter and headed for the door. "I hope that ends your investigating." She turned to look at me. "Leave the matter of finding the killer up to me."

I nodded and watched her go, hoping she didn't notice that I had my fingers crossed behind my back.

WHILE WILLA WAS busy out back with Gus, Pandora snuck out of the bookstore. She raced across the road to where she'd seen Snowball.

Skulking along, she followed the edge of the building to the back. It was wooded like a forest, but as she walked farther to the back, the trees seemed greener, the ferns larger, and the moss softer.

Snowball was standing atop the gray stones of a well. Pandora joined her, feeling warmth from the stones as she jumped atop them.

"Check this out." Snowball indicated for her to look into the well.

The iridescent water in the well swirled with magical energy. Pandora could feel her fur standing on end. It was like they were being charged with electricity.

"No wonder the plants in the shop grow so quickly," Pandora said. "Louise must use this water to nourish them."

"That might explain the real reason why she doesn't want the building demolished," Snowball said.

"Do you think she knows its power?" Pandora wondered. "And if she does, maybe she wants the amulet for good purposes."

"Maybe. It's not for us to decide, though. Even if she does want it for good, what if someone takes it from her?"

"Right. We need to report to the cats."

Snowball nodded. "We'll discuss it when we meet tonight at the barn. See you there."

Pandora headed back toward the bookstore, hoping she could slip back in before Willa noticed she was gone.

CHAPTER 10

I was stocking some poetry books when Pandora came trotting down the aisle. Her gray fur shone as she stretched then rubbed her face against the spines of several of the books on the shelf.

"I see you've been napping in one of your secret spots," I said. The cat often disappeared for hours. I didn't know where she hid, but sometimes, it seemed like she wasn't even in the shop.

"Careful with those books." The ghost of Robert Frost appeared, looking quite insulted that I'd let Pandora rub her cheek against one of his poetry books.

"Oh, quit whining." Franklin Pierce's ghost

swirled beside Robert. "Maybe if your books were better, they'd be on a higher shelf like mine."

"And maybe if your biographies weren't so boring, people would actually want to read them," Robert retorted then directed a stern ghostly gaze at Willa. "Your grandmother used to put my books on a much higher shelf."

"That's because she had to put them at eye level to remind people you even existed." Franklin smirked.

"Guys, I think people like both your books," I said as I relocated Robert's book to a higher shelf. "Sorry, Robert, I didn't mean to bottom-shelf you."

Robert looked slightly mollified. "I'll let it slide this time." Then he cocked his head to the left. "Oh, you have a customer."

I frowned. "There's no one in the shop but me and—"

Just then, the bells over the door jangled, and the two ghosts disappeared.

I poked my head out to see who had come in. It was two women who headed straight for the mystery aisle.

"Can I help you find anything?" I called over to them.

The taller of the two, a willowy brunette, turned and smiled at me. "We're just browsing," she said before turning back to the books.

Her companion, a redhead shorter than her by several inches, was already thumbing through one of the paperbacks on the shelf.

I left them to their browsing. In the short time I'd owned the bookstore, I'd noticed that people generally liked to be left alone when looking for a book. I knew I did. We had sofas and chairs for people to sit in if they wanted to read a chapter or two.

I was just about to go back to stocking books when the bells chimed again. This time, it was Althea Dunn. Clad in the same designer suit she always wore, the middle-aged woman had shoulder-length brown hair with a touch of silver and carried a large leather briefcase.

After Gus left, I'd called Althea to tell her the book she'd ordered, *Persuasion in Selling*, was in. Though from what I'd heard, she didn't really need to be more persuasive, or at least, her son didn't.

"Willa. Nice to see you. You left a message

that my book came in," she said in a clipped and not-too-friendly tone.

"Yes, indeed. It's right here on the counter," I replied cheerily and beckoned her to follow me to the register, where I'd stashed the copy of *Persuasion in Selling* on a shelf underneath. "I suppose you heard what happened here? I know you and Bradley were colleagues of sorts. Sorry for your loss."

Okay, I was shamelessly fishing for information, but I was sure Althea didn't know that.

"Colleagues? I don't know if I would say that," Althea said.

"Oh, I heard something about you and Grady working with him on the place across the street." I jutted my chin toward the plant store.

She turned to look out the window. "Yes, it is an eyesore, isn't it? But I wouldn't say we were working with Bradley. He's just an inspector."

"But your son would like to buy that building, I heard."

"I suppose he would. He's big on wanting to improve the town, but Dudley Chambers owns the building, and he's not interested in selling."

Althea took out her credit card and handed it to me.

I rang up the book. "That will be twelve dollars, please. Would you like a bag?"

"No, thanks, I'll put it in my briefcase," Althea replied as she took her credit card back and then shoved the book into her briefcase. "Thank you."

The two women who'd come in earlier approached the counter, each with a stack of books, as Althea exited the store.

"I don't think she needed a book on persuasion," the brunette said.

The redhead snorted. "You can say that again. Somehow, she and her son persuaded me to sell my old house."

"How did they do that?" I asked as I rang up her books.

"I'm not sure. They approached me about it and said I could get a lot of money." She shrugged. "I actually wasn't interested, but they talked me into having someone come out and inspect it."

I raised my brow but didn't ask if it was Bradley.

"It was a gorgeous antique house. One of

the oldest in the Notch." The brunette handed over her stack of books. "But that inspector said there was a major issue with the foundation, so it's probably good you sold it."

"I suppose." The redhead didn't look convinced. "Anyway, I have a nice condo with a great view now."

"That's right. Look at the positives!" her friend said.

They paid for the books and left. As I watched them go, I couldn't help but wonder if it was Bradley Ebert who had inspected the house, and if so, what did that all mean?

CHAPTER 11

That night, Pandora waited patiently while Willa ate her pizza and watched TV. Finally, the human went to bed, and Pandora snuck out and made a beeline to Elspeth's barn.

It was a clear night, and the moonlight shone bright into the barn, illuminating the square shapes of the bales of hay.

The cats came out of the shadows, all gathering around her.

"Snowball has told us about the magical stream at Petal Pushers," Inkspot informed her.

Pandora nodded. "Louise Franklin certainly had motive to kill Bradley Ebert. That stream has made her plants lusher and more vibrant. If she had to move, she would lose access to it."

The cats meowed their agreement, then Otis hopped up onto a bale of hay. Pandora figured he liked to stand up there so he could look down on them.

"One might assume that, but assumptions are not always correct," Otis said in his usual tone of smug superiority.

Pandora rolled her eyes. She hated when Otis acted like he was better than everyone else. But she couldn't deny that the cat did seem to have an uncanny ability to solve puzzles and sniff out trouble.

"Do you know something the rest of us don't?" Inkspot asked.

Otis nodded and addressed Inkspot. "I've been investigating as instructed and talked to the feral cats."

As his words rang through the barn, a small striped cat appeared out of nowhere and slinked toward them.

Pandora stared in surprise as the tiny feline approached, weaving back and forth between bales of hay with elegance. His fur was a bit scruffy, but he looked healthy otherwise. She recognized him as one of the feral cats that lived in a colony in the woods.

"The feral cats know a lot about what goes on in town," Otis explained. "And they tell me Louise could not have killed Bradley Eberts."

"How do they know that?" Snowball asked.

Otis paused for dramatic effect. "Because Louise was feeding the feral cats at the time of his death. Sebastian here will vouch for it."

Pandora sighed at the dramatics. "You could have just told us that instead of making a big production." Pandora turned to the little striped cat. "Thank you for coming, Sebastian."

"My pleasure," the cat purred.

"There is another person using magic in the town," Pandora said.

"Who?" Inkspot asked.

"I was able to peek into the backroom of the Mystic Spa today, and I saw a woman wearing a face mask that had a magical aura."

"Marina Bettencourt would benefit by amplifying the magic of her facials. It would get her more customers," Tigger said.

"And she was there early that morning. She even came out into the alley. Maybe she was the one who took the amulet and realized there was a shard missing. She might have been coming out to retrieve it."

"You should be able to get your human to investigate that," Otis said.

Pandora bristled. Otis always had to make a jab at how she couldn't communicate fully with Willa. She'd show him. "In fact, Willa did go to the spa this morning. I'm just waiting to find out what she discovered."

Pandora didn't add that she'd need to wait for Willa to tell someone since the telepathic communications she'd tried with her new human had yet to be successful. Maybe she shouldn't have left the bookstore when Gus showed up. Hopefully, she didn't miss anything important in Willa and Gus's conversation.

"Well?" Otis prompted.

"I'll get back to you," Pandora said.

"I hope it is Marina. That would be a fairly innocent use of the amulet." Snowball licked her paw and washed behind her ears.

"One can only hope," Tigger said.

"I did overhear something else of interest." Pandora told them about the woman who had claimed that Grady Dunn had persuaded her to sell her house. "It almost sounded like he used some magical powers to do that."

Otis frowned. "But why? To sell more houses and get more commissions?"

"I'm afraid it might be more sinister than that," Inkspot said. "Was the house an old house?"

"Yes. One of the oldest." Pandora had a bad feeling about where this was going.

Inkspot nodded. "I'm afraid someone might be gathering magical items that have been hidden in Mystic Notch for centuries. These items, when gathered together, could open a portal for evil forces."

The cats gasped.

"And the amulet is one of these items?" Tigger asked.

Inkspot nodded. "The items have been missing for two hundred years. Scattered throughout town and hidden by the elders long ago to prevent this from happening."

"And you think those items might be in the old houses?" Pandora asked. "Gus came to the bookstore this morning saying that Bradley's wife was complaining about the missing amulet. She said he'd found it in one of the old houses he inspected!"

Inkspot nodded. "Yes, indeed."

"If Bradley was the person collecting them, then the threat is over, as he is dead," Snowball said.

"But someone took the amulet," Otis pointed out. "And there may be more than one person. What if Bradley's wife is carrying on where he left off?"

"Or Grady Dunn is getting people to sell the houses so he has an excuse to look around inside. Bradley could have found the amulet by accident and taken it," Tigger said.

"Even Marina can't be ruled out. What if she is using the magical facials to get access to her clients' old homes? Does she offer to do house calls? She lives in the old Donnelly place, the oldest in town. Perhaps she bought it because she knew one of the relics was inside," Snowball said. "After all, she was at the scene."

"These are all good theories." Inkspot turned to Pandora. "Watch your human closely. If she is looking into this, she could be in danger."

CHAPTER 12

The next morning, I got to the bookstore early. I needed to tidy up a bit. I dusted the surfaces and plumped the pillows on the sofa then took out the trash.

After opening the back door, I stepped out hesitantly. I couldn't help but think about how I'd found Bradley dead out here just the other day. As I headed toward the dumpster, I saw movement out of the corner of my eye.

I dropped the trash bag and whirled around.

"Oh, sorry! Didn't mean to startle you." Grady Dunn held up his hands.

"It's okay," I said, my heart still pounding in

my chest. "I just didn't expect to see anyone back here."

"Yeah, sorry about that," Grady said sheepishly. "I was just emptying my trash." He gestured toward the dumpster.

"Here? Don't you have a dumpster at your building?"

"It's full." Grady started to back away. "They don't come to my place often enough."

"Ours gets pretty full too." I was a little peeved that he would just come over and use our dumpster. We paid for the service and didn't need him filling it up. But was that really why he was here?

I looked at him more closely, studying the way his jaw twitched and the way he kept glancing around nervously. There was something about this man that made me uneasy. What if he was the killer, coming back to the scene of the crime? Come to think of it, I hadn't heard the dumpster lid bang down, and he didn't have trash in his hand right now.

"Well, gotta run!" Grady headed out to the street.

I watched him leave then tossed my trash out and went inside to open the store.

By the time I got back in, the regulars were peering in the windows. I unlocked the door, and they filed in. Bing handed me a coffee.

"Thanks." I snapped open the plastic lid and took a sip while he bent to pet Pandora.

As usual, the cat rubbed against his legs and purred.

"What's new with you, Pandora?" he asked as if she were a person. She meowed, and his brow furrowed as if she'd said something he could understand and didn't particularly like.

The others took their places on the sofa and chairs.

"What's new with the investigation?" Hattie got right to the point, her blue eyes sparkling with excitement.

"Not much," I replied, sinking into my own favorite chair. "Gus hasn't mentioned anything, but then again, she wouldn't. Though I did just have something strange happen out back."

Bing's bushy brows rose. "Oh?"

"Grady Dunn was out there. He said he was using our dumpster, but I'm not so sure."

"Revisiting the scene of the crime," Cordelia said.

"I don't know. My money is on Marina." Josiah looked at us over the rim of his cup.

"Marina?" I frowned. "Gus seems to think she's in the clear."

"What else has Gus said?" Bing asked.

I sat back and took another sip of coffee. "Not much, but I did find out some interesting things on my own."

I told them about how I'd heard Louise Franklin yelling down at the town hall and how I'd tried to peek at Marina's sign-in book.

"That was sneaky of you." Bing looked like he was proud of me, and my cheeks heated.

"Unfortunately, I wasn't able to look at it."

"Interesting." Hattie fixed her gaze on me. "But not enough to base a murder investigation on, I'm afraid."

Cordelia leaned forward, her face alight with interest. "What about opportunity? Who had opportunity? We know Marina was here at that time."

"But we don't know where Grady or Louise were," Josiah said. "I can put some feelers out."

"There's something else," I said.

"What is it?" Hattie asked.

I hesitated, not sure if I should say

anything. Hopefully, Gus wouldn't be mad. "Gus came by looking for a necklace that Bradley's wife said he'd gotten from an old house he inspected. Apparently, he was wearing it the day he died, but it wasn't listed in his effects."

"You mean he was killed over a necklace?" Cordelia asked.

Bing almost choked on his coffee, and everyone turned to him.

"Are you okay?" I asked.

He waved his hand. "Fine. Wrong pipe." He leaned forward. "You were saying something about a necklace. Did Gus say what it looked like?"

I pressed my lips together, trying to remember. "About an inch-long pendant and shiny blue and green."

"Could Grady have been looking for that out back this morning?" Bing asked.

"I don't think so. He was over by the spa and not looking on the ground. At least, I didn't see him doing that, though who knows what he had been doing before I got out there." I sighed. "Speaking of Grady, there is another strange thing. Some women were in here yesterday, and Althea picked up a book she'd ordered. After she left, one of them practically accused Grady of forcing her to sell her house. She acted almost like he hypnotized her or something."

"Huh... was it an old house?" Bing asked.

"How did you know that?" I wondered.

"Just a guess."

The others looked at him in confusion, and he shrugged. "It could be a clue," he said.

"I think Louise is the most-likely suspect." Cordelia stood and straightened her lavender jacket. "Are you ready, Hattie? We need to get to the market. They are having a sale on hot dogs today, and we don't want to miss out."

Bing and Josiah stood too.

"I have to get home and rummage in my garage for my mushroom-digging equipment. I'm going to the woods in back of the old Wheeler house," Bing said.

"The one that's been abandoned for years?" Josiah asked.

"Yes, I'm going to be looking for hen of the woods mushrooms," Bing replied. "The trees there are really old, and there are lots of fallen logs, perfect for mushrooms to grow."

"That place is spooky," Cordelia said with a shudder. "I wouldn't go back there alone."

Bing just laughed. "I'm not afraid of ghosts, Cordelia." He glanced out into the bookstore, and my heart lurched. Could he see Robert and Franklin? I turned to look, but they weren't there.

"Anyway, I got permission from Grady to go back there."

"Grady is selling that one too?" I asked. "He seems to specialize in the old houses."

"Well, there are a ton of them in town," Josiah said.

"Have a great day, Willa," Hattie said and then glanced over at Petal Pushers. "And if you do any more investigating, make sure you be careful. Someone in town was willing to kill once, and they probably won't hesitate to do it again."

The inside of Petal Pushers was like a tropical jungle. Potted plants and floral arrangements covered every inch of the space. Vines climbed the walls and curled around the window frames. The musky scent of damp earth mingled pleasantly with the sweet aroma of the flowers. Humid air frizzed out my hair the minute I stepped inside.

Louise Franklin turned from a large potted palm that she had been watering. She was tall with eyes as green as the plants she cared for. Her blond hair hung down her back in a thick ponytail. She was wearing a loose white gauzy shirt and faded blue jeans. The first thing I looked for was a necklace like the one Gus had described. She wasn't wearing one. Of course, that didn't mean that she didn't have it at home.

"Oh, hi. Willa, right?" she said. I was afraid she might recognize me as the eavesdropper from the town hall, but if she did, her face didn't show it.

"Yes, I figured since I own the store across the street now, I'd come over and introduce myself properly."

She smiled and held out her hand to shake mine. "It's nice to meet you. I'm Louise. I was so sorry to hear about your grandmother's passing. I really liked her."

I pushed away a pang of sadness at the mention of my grandmother. "Thank you. I appreciate that. It's been tough, but I'm glad to be able to keep her store going."

She gave me a sympathetic smile. "That's good. I'd hate to see the bookstore close. It's a special place."

With two ghosts in residence, she didn't know the half of it!

"This place is great too," I said, looking around. "The plants are so vibrant. How long have you been here?"

"Ages." Louise stroked a giant plant leaf lovingly.

"I heard something about Bradley Eberts writing up some code violations? He wrote me up too."

Louise's expression hardened at the mention of Bradley. "Either he had no idea what he was doing, or he was lying." She pointed to the walls. "This building is old. He wrote up the cracks, saying it was a structural issue, but it's old horsehair plaster and has nothing to do with the structure," Louise said. "He also said the building didn't have proper exits, but there are three ways out of here.

"And he said the fire escape was inadequate." She showed me where the fire escape was. It looked okay to me.

"Those don't seem like things that would cause the building to be condemned. Why would he do that?" I asked.

She crossed her arms over her chest. "You tell me. I think Bradley was up to something with those real estate people, but I'm not sure what or why."

"I heard Grady wanted to buy this building

and tear the place down for a shiny new real estate office."

"He did, but I've worked hard to build a business here and would hate to move," Louise said. "Anyway, I don't think Dudley, the owner, is interested in selling. He's focusing on his properties in Florida."

"Did you notice anything odd the morning Bradley was killed?" I figured it was a fair question since her store was right across the street, but it was really a sneaky way to find out if she was near the scene of the crime. It would have been easy to kill him in the alley and then sneak back over here.

Her eyes flicked away. "Oh, ummm... I was out."

"Oh? I guess it's kind of early for you to be open," I prompted, hoping for more information. She sure did seem evasive now.

"Yes," she said a little too quickly. Then she let out a nervous laugh, and her eyes flicked over to my store. "You're a cat lover, right?"

I turned to see Pandora snoozing in her bed. "Yes. Sort of. Pandora was Gram's cat."

Louise nodded as if making up her mind. "I

was out feeding the feral cats that morning. There's a group of us that takes care of them."

I was intrigued. "Really? How many do you have?" I asked, feeling a sudden rush of compassion for the strays.

"About a dozen or so," Louise said with a sigh, her eyes growing distant as she seemed to remember something from long ago. "Some of them were so thin when I first started, but now there are a bunch of us that make sure they get food and medical attention."

"Oh, wow, that's so nice," I said, full of admiration.

"We're always looking for new helpers," she said hopefully. "But I'll have to ask you not to tell anyone, because some people in town want to harm the cats, and we don't want them to know their location."

"Thanks, I'll think about that. And I promise I won't mention it to a soul." I paused. "So, you have no idea what Bradley was up to or who would want to kill him?"

Louise shook her head. "Probably a lot of folks might not like him, but to kill him? That would be another level. Maybe his wife? The spouse is usually the main suspect, aren't they?"

"They are, but Bradley was into something weird. You said so yourself."

"Yeah, true."

"You know what the weirdest thing was? Grady had him inspecting the houses for the sellers. He came here before they even approached Dudley to sell." Louise shook her head. "That's not how it usually works. The seller puts the property up, and *then* the buyer pays for an inspection. I wonder if that was the scam. Finding something 'fake' wrong with the house so that the sellers want to dump it? He takes a commission on all these sales."

"And that might explain why he sells a lot of old houses. People won't be so suspicious that something is wrong."

"But now that Bradley is dead, I guess that puts a damper on his little scheme unless he can train the new inspector to be in on it." Louise pressed her lips together. "I guess that also eliminates Grady as a suspect in his murder."

"I guess so. Unless Bradley threatened to expose Grady, and that's why he was killed."

CHAPTER 14

I went back to my store, but my mind kept going back to Grady and his con. I wondered if Bradley had been blackmailing him. That might be why he was killed. Too bad I couldn't get any of that info from Gus.

I talked out loud to the cat as she stared at me from her cat bed. She was a good listener. I actually felt like she understood.

"I wonder how I can find out if Bradley came into money." I put another Western paperback on top of the pile. "I suppose Gus won't tell me."

"Meow!" Pandora's tone indicated that she didn't think so either.

"That bit about his necklace being missing is weird too." I picked up a pile of books and headed toward the stacks.

"Mew." Pandora had followed right behind me. She looked up at me expectantly. She probably wanted to be fed.

"I think maybe Bradley was killed over something he knew," I said to Pandora as I put another book on the shelf. "That's usually what it is if it isn't the spouse. I'm sure Gus must have checked her out by now, though."

Pandora just looked at me and meowed, but she seemed to be agreeing with me.

I furrowed my brow in concentration. "Miranda might have been lying when she said she had a client."

"Meow!" Pandora batted at a book on the shelf. Luckily, it wasn't one of Robert's poetry books or Franklin's biographies. They took a dim view of cat scratches on their leather bindings.

I headed toward the cookbook aisle. "Louise might have been lying too. She seemed sincere, but I wonder if anyone can vouch for her feeding the feral cats."

"Meow!" Pandora seemed to almost nod her head. Weird.

"Grady was seen at the scene of the crime this morning. I don't believe his story about using the trash. Maybe I should check his dumpster."

"Meow." Pandora swished her tail back and forth.

"The bit with the old houses is really strange. My journalistic instincts tell me there is something there."

I sighed and grabbed my purse. It was the slow time of day, and if I was going to check out Grady's dumpster, this would be a good time. The garbage truck came tomorrow.

Gus had said she didn't have much experience dealing with this sort of thing, but I had years of it. Not as a cop, but I'd still done a fair amount of investigating and worked with many officers. I hadn't been around for my sister the past few decades. Maybe I could make up for that by helping her out, whether she wanted me to or not.

PANDORA FELT worry settle over her as she watched Willa go off toward the real estate office. She'd tried to discuss the clues with her human, but Willa seemed unable to understand her body language and telepathic communications. Too bad, because Willa had gotten some things wrong, and now she'd run off to investigate.

Pandora stretched and jumped off the counter. She hoped Willa didn't continue to pursue the theory that Bradley was killed because he knew something. Pandora was sure that the real reason was that he was killed because he *possessed* something that someone else wanted. Not that she could have told Willa that. Willa wasn't advanced enough yet to understand about magical amulets and witches.

She had been right to suspect that Miranda was lying, though. Miranda was magical and would have wanted the amulet. Pandora had confirmed as much with her feline senses—though she had no idea whether or not Miranda really did have a client that morning.

Pandora sighed as she watched Willa walk

down the street. She was sure the human would mess things up without her help.

Pandora headed for her secret escape route inside the bookstore. She figured Willa would need her help sooner rather than later. The human was bound to stumble without Pandora's guidance.

I TOOK a circuitous route to the real estate office because I didn't want Grady to see me approaching. I slipped around back. The dumpster was on the side of the parking lot and hidden from view by a fenced-in area. I looked around to see if there were any security cameras. None were visible, so I opened the door to the fence slowly, careful not to make any sounds, and went in.

The dumpster was a medium size. The metal was stained with rust, the lid discolored and dented, with a crack running through its middle. The smell of rotting food and other things I didn't even want to consider assaulted my nostrils. I covered my nose and clenched my teeth as I cautiously lifted the lid.

I was expecting the dumpster to be overflowing since he had said he'd had to use ours because this one was full. Surely, the trash would at least reach nearly to the top. But when I lifted the lid, I saw it was half empty!

Suddenly, the back door to the real estate office opened. I crouched down, holding my breath.

"I'm going to the old Wheeler house," Grady said, jangling his keys. "I don't want to be disturbed."

"Okay, Mr. Dunn," someone yelled out the door as it slammed shut.

My heart raced as I peeked through the slats in the fence to see him get into a silver Lexus and drive away. I waited a few moments before scurrying out of the dumpster area and running to my own car.

If Grady was up to something at that old house, now would be a good time to catch him at it.

CHAPTER 15

The Lexus that Grady had driven away from the real estate office was in the driveway of the Wheeler house, along with a Hyundai that had a dinged-up fender. Had they replaced Bradley, and was Grady already getting the replacement in on his scam?

I parked farther down the road and snuck in through the woods. My plan was to skulk around outside the house and see if I could see or overhear anything incriminating. I had my phone out so I could record or take pictures just in case I got lucky.

As I crept closer to the house, sounds of

scraping filled the air. It sounded like someone was down in the basement, rummaging around. I peered inside the low window and saw Grady in the corner of the basement. It looked like he was digging around the large granite stones.

Just then, my phone vibrated. It was a series of texts from Gus.

LEAVE THE SUSPECTS ALONE.

I saw you following Grady and heard you were interrogating Louise.

Grady didn't do it—he was at the Mystic Spa at the time of death, so back off!

GRADY GOES TO THE SPA? Was that why I saw him out back this morning? Clearly, that wasn't common knowledge. Maybe he went in the back door so no one would see. If it wasn't Grady and it wasn't Marina, then who had killed Bradley? And what was Grady doing in the basement? And where was the person that belonged to the other car?

"What do you think you're doing here? Are you snooping around?"

My heart jerked, and I turned to see Althea standing behind me, her hands on her hips and a scowl on her face.

"I, umm… I was meeting Bing here to pick mushrooms." I glanced into the woods, hoping to see signs of Bing.

"You were? The path isn't anywhere near here." Althea looked skeptical.

"Right. Well, I'll just be going…" I started to back away, and that's when I noticed her necklace. It was exactly as Gus had described. A piece hung from a rawhide strip, was oval in shape, and glowed almost as if it had a light source inside it. It was so vivid that I couldn't stop staring at the blueish-green glow.

Althea touched the necklace as if trying to hide it. "You're not really here for mushrooms, are you?"

She started toward me, and I remembered the phone in my hand. I had to send a message to Gus. But before I could type more than a few letters, she grabbed the phone away from me.

"Sorry, Willa. I can't let you text anyone now. Since you're nosey enough to want to know what's going on and you won't be able to tell anyone, I might as well fill you in." She leaned closer, and I could see the madness in her eyes. "I was the one who killed Bradley."

"You did? But why? Is it something to do with the houses? Did he discover your scam and try to blackmail you?"

She sneered. "Something like that."

Aha! I'd figured it out. Fat lot of good that was going to do me now. It didn't appear as if Althea was going to let me live long enough to tell anyone.

"Let's go for a walk, shall we?" she said in a voice that was more of a snarl. Her clawlike hand clamped onto my upper arm, and she dragged me toward the back of the house.

In the back of the house was a big stone well. I had a bad feeling about this. I scanned the woods, trying to find a path. I had to make a break for it.

I broke loose and dashed toward the trees, but Althea was too fast. How a middle-aged woman like her had such speed was a wonder. She grabbed me from behind and spun me around, her hand on my mouth to silence any screams.

My eyes widened as she pushed me toward the well. The necklace seemed to glow even more. She shoved my upper body over the edge of the well. She was going to push me in! Even though I put up my best struggle, she was winning. My arms flailed backward, trying to hold on to anything. They finally found the necklace, and I yanked, causing Althea to loosen her hold on me.

Then suddenly, I heard a loud crack followed by a scream of pain, and she let go. I jumped back and turned around to see Althea lying on the ground, a big stone next to her and Grady staring down at her.

"You hit her?"

Grady looked up, his eyes wild. "I had to. She was trying to push you in the well. She's been acting so strange lately."

Grady picked up the necklace, which had fallen beside the well when I'd pulled it off, and looked closely at it. His face paled. "This is Bradley's necklace."

"I think she might have killed him," I said.

Grady dissolved into tears. "I knew she was acting strange, but I never imagined..."

We looked at each other, and I could see the sadness in his eyes.

A siren blared in the distance, bringing us back to reality. Was that Gus? I grabbed my phone and jotted off a message as Grady knelt beside his mother.

"She's still breathing." He sounded relieved.

A noise over by the woods drew our attention, and I turned to see Bing with a basket of mushrooms in his hand. His brows drew together. "What in the world is going on here?"'

"She was trying to kill Willa. I had to stop her," Grady explained.

"She killed Bradley. That's his necklace." I pointed to the necklace in Grady's hand.

Bing's eyes widened. He put down the basket and came toward us.

"Althea is the killer?" Bing asked and took the necklace from Grady's hands. He held it close to his face and frowned. "I think this is evidence. We'd better not get fingerprints on it." Bing fumbled around in his pocket then brought out a tissue to hold the necklace with.

I noticed it did not glow as brightly as before. Odd. "Why would your mother kill Bradley?"

Grady shook his head. "I should have said something sooner. I think she had some kind of an agreement with Bradley to exaggerate things wrong with these old houses. I guess she wanted more sales. I suspected... but I couldn't let myself believe there was something illegal going on. "I was actually just in the basement, trying to see if I could figure out what they were up to. I'd seen Bradley doing something strange down there the other day. I had no idea my mother was even here."

"But why would she kill him if they had an agreement?" I asked.

Grady looked down at Althea, who was starting to wake up. "I think Bradley got greedy. She was withdrawing a lot of money from the bank lately. He might have been blackmailing her."

Movement in the woods caught my eye again, and I saw gray fur and a tail.

"Wait. Is that Pandora?" I strained to see, but whatever it was ducked behind a tree.

"I'll go see." Bing raced off toward the

woods just as the sound of tires squealing out front announced the arrival of the police.

"What's going on here?" Gus demanded, looking at Althea sprawled on the ground and then at me, Grady, and Bing, who had returned from checking on the cat.

Grady explained how Althea had killed Bradley and then tried to kill me.

"She had this necklace." Bing held up the evidence then looked over at me. "That wasn't Pandora, just one of the feral cats."

Gus gestured for one of her deputies to take care of a groaning Althea, then she lowered her gun and took the necklace. "This matches the description that Bradley's wife gave me."

That explained a lot, but there was still one question no one had answered. I turned to Gus. "How did you know I was here and in trouble?"

Gus rolled her eyes. "After I sent you the warning text, you replied with some random nonsense. I figured something was wrong. I knew you had followed Grady, so I stopped in at the real estate office to see where he went."

"Oh, well... I'm glad you showed up. I guess." We'd had the situation under control, but maybe it was good she'd shown up before

Althea had fully woken up. She was proving to be a bit of a handful to Gus's deputy, who was hauling her to her feet.

"Let's get her downtown. I'll get an official confession at the station." Gus indicated for the deputy to take Althea away, then she turned to me. "Don't look so pleased with yourself. You never should have been here butting in. I'll deal with you later."

Pandora raced through the forest, her paws pounding the earth that was covered in layers of leaves. The tall oaks towered above her as the pungent scents of pine, earth, and moss mingled with the melodies of birds singing and the rustling of squirrels and chipmunks foraging for food.

The amulet that Bing had handed her was warm in her mouth. She wasn't sure how he'd managed to pull that off. Somehow, he'd replaced the real amulet with a fake when he'd gotten the tissue out of his pocket. Being a magician, he could pull off the presto-chango part easily, but had he been carrying the fake one the whole time just in case?

Pandora didn't have time to ponder that. She was on a mission, the amulet heavy in her mouth as she pressed on toward Elspeth's barn.

She burst through the doors of Elspeth's barn and dropped the amulet at Inkspot's feet. The cats gathered around, listening intently as Pandora told them how Althea had been the one to kill Bradley.

"Bing managed to replace the enchanted amulet with a nonenchanted version so that Gus would have the evidence to arrest her," Pandora said.

"That's good work," Inkspot said.

"Thanks. They're taking Althea into the police station now," Pandora added.

"But why? Gus couldn't possibly know that she was collecting magical relics. She doesn't know there's magic here in the Notch." Snowball swished her tail.

"Grady said that she was running a real estate scam with Bradley. I guess Bradley got greedy and tried to blackmail her," Pandora said. "At least, that's what the humans believe."

"I think that might be partly true," Tigger said. "Bradley wasn't magical, so he must have gotten lucky and found the amulet in one of the houses, and Althea wanted it. I bet that is the real reason she killed him."

Inkspot nodded. "And she was likely collecting enchanted items from all the old houses. She probably has more, and we need to get them and give them to Elspeth for safe-keeping."

"If she's at the police station now, her place is empty. I can run over there and see what else she has," Otis volunteered. The magical cats could sniff out enchanted objects, and Otis was a master at finding his way into houses. If anyone could retrieve the objects, he could. Pandora had to at least give him credit for that.

Otis hopped down from his perch atop the bale of hay and trotted off.

"It's good that the humans think there is a nonmagical reason to arrest Althea," Inkspot said. "If she's in jail, she can't harm anyone with evil magic."

"But we know the truth," Tigger said solemnly.

Inkspot nodded. "And once again, we've saved the Notch, thanks to Pandora."

"SO, ALTHEA CONFESSED TO KILLING BRADLEY?" I picked a pepperoni off the pizza that Gus had brought over to my house for supper. Was this some sort of peace offering? Maybe it was Gus's way of apologizing for being so hard on me about intervening in the case. I was sure I'd helped solve it but would never say that to Gus.

"Yep." Gus wiped a blob of sauce from her chin. "Apparently, Althea had been paying Bradley to write up fake inspections noting the houses had major damage. Then she'd convince the owners to sell to her. They'd think they were getting out of a big problem. Althea told them she could fix the problems at cost, so it was worth it for her. Then she'd sell at a high price."

"Huh." I nodded. This was exactly what I'd suspected. "Sounds like a good deal. What went wrong?"

Gus shrugged. "Bradley got greedy, and Althea didn't want to pay his blackmail price."

"Mew!" Pandora said, raising her head and staring at us with those intelligent golden-green eyes. She had been watching us talk as if she was part of the conversation.

Gus's hand hovered over the pizza. "Do cats like pepperoni?"

"I don't think it's good for them." I glanced at Pandora's bowl, which was full of kibble. "You have plenty of food, Pandora."

Pandora looked back at the bowl and frowned.

"What about Grady? Are you charging him with anything?" I asked.

Gus shook her head. "There's no evidence that he knew what Althea was up to. He was quite upset about the whole thing."

I frowned. "Really? But they worked in the real estate business together. Kind of hard not to notice."

Gus shrugged. "Maybe he chose not to see what was going on. I think maybe he just didn't want to believe it. I guess when it's family, you want to believe the best of them."

Our eyes met over the pizza, and we both smiled.

I grabbed another slice and folded it in half, thinking about Grady's predicament. All this time, he had probably suspected his mom was up to something shady, but he chose to ignore it.

"Well," Gus said, "at least this case is solved. Should be an easy conviction. But still, I can't help but feel there's more to it."

"Mew!" Pandora rubbed her face against my ankles.

"She must really like pizza," Gus said then looked at me sternly. "No more investigating on your own, okay? You could have gotten hurt this time."

I nodded even though I secretly wondered if Gus would have solved the case without me. Had Gus even suspected Althea? I didn't dare ask.

"Don't worry. I have no intention of confronting a killer again. Besides, what are the odds there would ever be another murder here in Mystic Notch?"

"Meow!" Pandora practically shrieked, and we both turned to look at her.

Gus laughed. "Well, that sound rather ominous."

"It sure did. I hope she doesn't know something we don't know." I joked, but I had to wonder...

OF COURSE, Pandora does know more than Willa and Gus, and there will be another murder. And another.. and another.... Save 30% on the first 8 full length books in the series when you buy the bundle in my store:

GET 30% Off Mystic Notch Books 1-8 -> Click Here

OR

Buy book 1, Ghostly Paws, at your favorite retailer:

A MYSTIC NOTCH COZY MYSTERY
BOOK ONE
GHOSTLY
PAWS
USA TODAY BESTSELLING AUTHOR
LEIGHANN DOBBS

Paws and Effect

Probable Paws

A Whisker of a Doubt

Wrong Side of the Claw

Claw and Order

Juniper Holiday Cozy Mysteries

***

Halloween Party Murder

Thanksgiving Dinner Death

Who Slayed The Santas?

Masquerade Party Murder

My Fatal Valentine

Oyster Cove Guesthouse

Cat Cozy Mystery Series

***

A Twist in the Tail

A Whisker in the Dark

A Purrfect Alibi

Kate Diamond Mystery Adventures

***

Hidden Agemda (Book 1)

Ancient Hiss Story (Book 2)

Heist Society (Book 3)

Silver Hollow

Paranormal Cozy Mystery Series

***

A Spell of Trouble (Book 1)

Spell Disaster (Book 2)

Nothing to Croak About (Book 3)

Cry Wolf (Book 4)

Shear Magic (Book 5)

Mooseamuck Island

Cozy Mystery Series

* * *

A Zen For Murder

A Crabby Killer

A Treacherous Treasure

Blackmoore Sisters

Cozy Mystery Series

* * *

Dead Wrong

Dead & Buried

Dead Tide

Buried Secrets

Deadly Intentions

A Grave Mistake

Spell Found

Fatal Fortune

Hidden Secrets

Celestial Chaos

Lexy Baker

Cozy Mystery Series

* * *

Killer Cupcakes

Dying For Danish

Murder, Money and Marzipan

3 Bodies and a Biscotti

Brownies, Bodies & Bad Guys

Bake, Battle & Roll

Wedded Blintz

Scones, Skulls & Scams

Ice Cream Murder

Mummified Meringues

Brutal Brulee (Novella)

No Scone Unturned

Cream Puff Killer

Never Say Pie

Ain't Seen Muffin Yet

Assault and Buttercream

Lady Katherine Regency Mysteries

***

An Invitation to Murder (Book 1)

The Baffling Burglaries of Bath (Book 2)

Murder at the Ice Ball (Book 3)

A Murderous Affair (Book 4)

Murder on Charles Street (Book 5)

Julia and Nora Marsh 1920s Cozy Mystery

***

Murder on a Mississippi Steamboat

Hazel Martin Historical Mystery Series

***

Murder at Lowry House (book 1)

Murder by Misunderstanding (book 2)

Sam Mason Mysteries

(As L. A. Dobbs)

***

Telling Lies (Book 1)

Keeping Secrets (Book 2)

Exposing Truths (Book 3)

Betraying Trust (Book 4)

Killing Dreams (Book 5)

More books in the Rockford Security Series:

Cold As Her Heart

A Game of Kill

No One To Trust

No Time To Run

Don't Fear The Truth

Hide From The Past

Romantic Comedy

***

Corporate Chaos Series

In Over Her Head (book 1)

Can't Stand the Heat (book 2)

What Goes Around Comes Around (book 3)

Careful What You Wish For (4)

Dish Best Served Cold (5)

Contemporary Romance

***

Reluctant Romance

Sweet Romance (Written As Annie Dobbs)

Firefly Inn Series

***

Another Chance (Book 1)

Another Wish (Book 2)

Hometown Hearts Series

***

No Getting Over You (Book 1)

A Change of Heart (Book 2)

Sweet Mountain Billionaires

***

Jaded Billionaire (Book 1)

A Billion Reasons Not To Fall In Love (Book 2)

❊❊❊

Sweetrock Sweet and Spicy Cowboy Romance

Some Like It Hot

Too Close For Comfort

———

Regency Romance

❊ ❊ ❊

Scandals and Spies Series:

Kissing The Enemy

Deceiving the Duke

Tempting the Rival

Charming the Spy

Pursuing the Traitor

Captivating the Captain

The Unexpected Series:

An Unexpected Proposal

An Unexpected Passion

Dobbs Fancytales:

Dobbs Fancytales Boxed Set Collection

———

Western Historical Romance

***

Goldwater Creek Mail Order Brides:

Faith

American Mail Order Brides Series:

Chevonne: Bride of Oklahoma

Magical Romance with a Touch of Mystery

***

Something Magical

Curiously Enchanted

ABOUT THE AUTHOR

Leighann Dobbs discovered her passion for writing after a twenty year career as a software engineer. She lives in New Hampshire with her husband Bruce, their trusty Chihuahua mix Mojo and beautiful rescue cat, Kitty. When she's not reading, gardening or selling antiques, she likes to write romance and cozy mystery novels and novelettes which are perfect for the busy person on the go.

Connect with Leighann on Facebook and Twitter

http://facebook.com/leighanndobbsbooks

www.ingramcontent.com/pod-product-compliance
Lightning Source LLC
Chambersburg PA
CBHW071941210726
48293CB00004BA/1354